My Magical Pony

Red Skies

By Jenny Oldfield

Illustrated by Gillian Martin

Hodder
Children's
Books

A division of Hachette Children's Books

Chapter One

Krista worked hard all weekend. She mucked out stables and cleaned tack. She held the ponies steady as the blacksmith fitted new shoes then exercised Frankie in the arena and watched Jo put a saddle on the chestnut foal for the very first time.

"Good boy!" she murmured as Frankie had shifted his feet uneasily. "It's not going to hurt you. No one will do anything bad!"

Frankie nuzzled Krista's hand, then turned to look at the strange weight on his back. He sniffed it and decided that it was OK.

My Magical Pony

"See!" she soothed. "It's not nasty at all!"

Finally, it was the end of another busy day.
"I'm s-o-o-o tired!" she sighed. She leaned
against Comanche's stable door, looking up at
a bright blue sky.

The yard was empty except for her and the
piebald pony. The others were out in the fields.

Red Skies

"My legs ache, I've got blisters on my hands, and I'm starving!"

Comanche nudged her gently with his nose.

Krista smiled. "Yeah, I know – you want to go and eat grass with the rest of them!"

Friendly Comanche nudged her again. *Relax!* he seemed to say. *You've worked hard enough. Just chill out!*

Krista stroked his cheek. "I'm not complaining," she assured him. "There's nothing else in the world I'd rather be doing than working here, helping Jo out. You know that, don't you?"

This time Comanche lowered his head and snorted. His thick brown mane fell over his eyes. *Yeah, but it can't be all work and no play,*

he seemed to remind her.

Krista put her arms around his neck, gave him a hug and leaned her face against him. "You know what I'd love to do right now?" she murmured.

The little piebald shook his head and gave a soft, whickering sound.

"I'd love to put a saddle on your back and hack out along the cliff path," Krista went on. "We'd have the breeze in our hair and we'd ride down to the beach and have an evening gallop. How cool does that sound?"

"That sounds like a great idea," a voice interrupted.

Krista jumped and stood up straight. She saw Jo standing nearby. "Oops, I didn't

know you were there!" she cried.

Jo grinned. "Seriously, Krista. Why not take Comanche down to the beach? It'll do you both good."

"Wow!" Krista's eyes opened wide. "Do you mean it? Can I really? You're sure Comanche isn't too tired?"

"Go!" Jo insisted, hands on hips. "Take a break. If anyone deserves it, you do."

"Will you ring and tell Mum I'll be a bit late?" Krista checked. "And can you ask her to feed Spike for me?"

Spike was Krista's pet hedgehog. He would be waiting for his supper on the lawn at High Point.

Jo nodded twice. "Now go!" she ordered

again, still smiling as Krista dashed across the yard to the tack room and came back carrying Comanche's saddle and bridle.

Quickly Krista tacked up the pony and stepped up into the saddle. "Thanks, Jo!" she said with a broad smile. "I am so going to enjoy this ride!"

"Hey, Comanche, what was that?" Krista murmured.

The little pony had shied away from something hidden amongst the heather on the steep hill leading down to the beach. But he'd soon steadied himself and plodded calmly on.

"Probably a rabbit or a bird," Krista decided. She tightened the reins and urged Comanche

forward. "Just an itsy-bitsy tiny creature trying
to get away from your giant feet!"

She gazed down
on the wide expanse
of sand, humming a
tune. *How cool is this!*
she thought. *I am
so-o-o-o lucky!*

The sure-footed
pony soon reached
the bottom of the
hill and stepped out
on to the beach. Ahead of them, Whitton Bay
stretched towards Black Point. The tide was
going out, leaving a long expanse of solid,
wet sand for them to gallop along.

My Magical Pony

"Fancy a sprint along here?" Krista asked.

Comanche pricked up his ears. He had the salty scent of the sea in his nostrils as he swished his tail back and forth.

"Yeah, I guess you do!" Krista grinned. She pressed her legs against his flanks, sat deep in the saddle and urged him through trot and canter into a full-on gallop.

Comanche surged forward, his thick mane flying back, his feet thundering along the edge of the waves. He was loving every second, still gathering speed as he splashed through shallow water and kicked up spray behind him.

"Wow!" Krista murmured. She loved this sense of freedom, and the feeling that there was nothing else in the world except herself,

Red Skies

Comanche, the waves and the wind.

At last they came to the first rocks at the far end of Whitton Bay. "Whoa!" Krista said, gently pulling on the reins and settling her weight back into the saddle. The gallop was over.

Comanche put on the brakes and settled back into a walk. He strode boldly between the rocks, feeling the small waves whirl around his hooves.

"Cool!" Krista sighed, leaning forward to pat his neck. "You're so good, Commy, I love you to bits!"

Of all the ponies at Hartfell, Comanche was the most willing and reliable. He was solid and plucky. He never put a foot wrong.

13

In reply, the stocky piebald ducked his head and snorted. He turned away from the rocks, ready to face the gallop back along the sands to the point where they'd started.

Krista smiled. "Don't even think about it!" The pony's sides were heaving in and out. He was breathing heavily. "You and I are going to walk back!"

Comanche tossed his head. He pranced through the shallow waves. "Let's go for it!" he seemed to say.

"No, you need a rest," Krista insisted. She walked him steadily along the beach.

Behind them, the sun was sinking over the sea, turning red as it met the flat, shimmering horizon. Krista and Comanche's long shadow

14

stretched far across the wet sand.

"Perfect!" Krista sighed. Jo had been right – this was exactly what she'd needed.

Instead of taking the steep route back up the hillside, Krista decided to choose a different way home to Hartfell. "Let's go though the town,"

she told Comanche, steering him off the beach before they came to the cliff path. She knew that the streets of Whitton would not be busy at this time on a Sunday evening. "The hill's less steep if we go along the road."

Willing as ever, Comanche trod across the soft, dry sand towards the short promenade. They passed a couple of kids building sandcastles and Krista waved when they yelled a greeting. She stopped and let them fuss and pat Comanche.

"We have to go now," Krista told them, aware that the sun had almost set. It would take her half an hour to get back to the stables, and by that time it would be almost dark.

"OK, let's go!" she murmured, setting off at

16

a trot. It had probably been a mistake to stop
and talk. Now they were short of time and
they would have to hurry.

Comanche's metal shoes rang out in the
calm evening air. They trotted past the houses
overlooking the bay then took a right turn on
to a narrow, winding lane that would lead up
the hill to Hartfell.

Krista rose neatly to the trot, up and down
in the saddle. She could see over the high
walls into the neighbouring fields where
sheep grazed and new lambs played. Sweet!
she thought, glimpsing two white lambs
frisking on top of a small hillock.

Then, out of nowhere, a car engine roared
and a Land Rover appeared round the bend.

It rattled and swerved wide, heading towards Krista and Comanche on the wrong side of the road.

Krista gasped and reined Comanche back. There was no room to pass the car and trailer, still hurtling towards them.

Nightmare! They were going to crash! There was nothing Krista could do to stop it.

Stupid idiot! Krista thought, her throat constricted, her heart thumping.

The car driver saw the pony and rider then slammed on the brakes. There was a squeal of tyres from the Land Rover, the trailer slewed sideways across Comanche's path.

Poor Comanche reared and plunged sideways on to the narrow grass verge.

18

He crashed into the wall and flung Krista out of the saddle.

She tumbled over the wall into the field, losing sight of what was happening on the road.

Krista groaned. Her shoulder and left leg hurt, but she got straight up from the ground and limped back to the wall. "Comanche!" she gasped.

On the other side of the wall, car tyres squealed, the pony reared again with a shrill and terrified neigh.

"Oh please!" Krista cried, climbing the wall to get back into the lane. "Please don't let him be hurt! Please let him be OK!"

Chapter Two

The scene that greeted Krista filled her with dismay. The Land Rover was out of control, skidding towards the wall she had just climbed. Comanche was on the grass verge, down on his knees and struggling to stand. Meanwhile, the trailer swung towards him, swaying dangerously as it skidded across the lane.

Krista cried out.

The driver spun the steering wheel to avoid the wall, but the Land Rover scraped against the rough stones, smashing a headlight. The trailer towered over

Comanche, who at last struggled to his feet.

"Get out of the way, Commy!" Krista yelled, ducking to avoid the shower of splintering glass.

Too late – the trailer swung sideways into the pony, knocking him off balance and sending him crashing to the ground again.

"Oh no!" For a split second Krista closed her eyes. When she opened them again, the driver of the Land Rover had pulled away from the wall and was speeding on along the lane. The empty trailer swayed on its two wheels but kept upright. A second later, both car and trailer had vanished round the bend.

"Comanche!" Krista gasped, jumping down from the wall into the lane.

My Magical Pony

The pony had stopped neighing and made it back on to his feet. He was shaking from head to foot. There was a long red gash across his white face.

"You're bleeding!" she cried, reaching out to grab his trailing rein.

Terror showed in the whites of Comanche's eyes. His ears were laid flat against his head, he was frothing at the mouth.

"Steady – stand still!" Krista begged, lunging to catch the rein.

But the pony was out of his mind with fear. He reared up in the lane and pawed the air with his hooves. They crashed down close to Krista, who fell back on to the verge to avoid them.

"Stand!" she gasped, trying again.

Comanche reared a second time and swerved out of reach. Blood ran from the long cut on his nose, his eyes still rolled, his hooves clattered on to the tarmac.

Then he heard another car approaching. The sound of the engine sent him into a fresh panic.

Once more Krista cried out and ran ahead

down the lane. She stood in the road, waving both arms over her head to warn the driver of the sports car, which braked and slid to a halt.

Meanwhile, Comanche had decided to bolt. With a supreme effort he'd launched himself at the high wall and cleared it. By the time Krista had stopped the second car, he was galloping at full speed across the field where the sheep and lambs grazed.

"Watch what you're doing!" The man driving the sports car leaned out of his window and yelled at Krista. "Do you want to get yourself killed?"

"My pony!" she gasped. "We were in an accident. He's been injured!"

24

The man frowned. "Is that him, galloping up the hill?"

Krista nodded. "He got hit by the trailer. He's bleeding." She could hardly breathe, tears were streaming down her face.

The man, who was middle aged and wearing jeans and a brown suede jacket, got out of his car to examine the tyre marks and shattered glass. "Nasty," he muttered. "Are you sure you're OK?"

Krista nodded. "It was my fault," she stammered. "I should have been watching what I was doing."

"No, it looks like the driver was in too much of a hurry," the man argued, checking to see that Krista was only scared and not

seriously hurt. "She hurtled past me with her
trailer on the straight stretch of road back

there."

"What am I
going to do about
Comanche?" Krista
cried. By now he'd
galloped out of
sight, still in a panic
and no doubt still
bleeding badly.

"Is there someone I can call?" the man
asked. He took out his phone and listened
while Krista gave him Jo's name and number.

"Yes, I know her," the man replied. "She
belongs to the same tennis club as me."

Red Skies

"She's Comanche's owner," Krista explained. "What am I going to tell her?"

"Leave it to me." He waited a while and then spoke. "Hello, is that Jo Weston? It's Richard Bradley – from the tennis club. Yes. Listen, I'm afraid there's been an accident …"

"Let me speak!" Krista pleaded. She knew she should be the one to tell Jo the bad news. "Jo, it's me, Krista. I was riding Comanche along the lane out of Whitton. A car crashed into us. Comanche ran away."

There was a pause before Jo spoke. She was obviously making an effort to sound calm. "First things first. Are you all right, Krista?"

"I hurt my shoulder and my ankle, but it's not bad. It's Comanche I'm worried about.

He got cut on the face and ran off in a panic." Staring fearfully across the field where Comanche had fled, Krista could hardly force the words out.

"Don't worry about Comanche. He'll come to his senses and head for home." Jo did her best to calm Krista down. "Everything will be fine so long as you're OK."

"I don't know who it was or why she was driving so fast," Krista gabbled. "She came right at us, flying round the bend on the wrong side of the road …"

"Krista, don't worry. Just get yourself back here in one piece." Jo insisted on her handing the phone back to Richard.

He listened and nodded. "Sure," he said.

Red Skies

"No problem. I'll do that." Then he put the phone back in his pocket. "Come on, I'll drive you back to Hartfell," he told Krista.

"But what about Comanche?" she cried. "We have to stay here and find him!"

"No, we have to get you back. Jo is planning to call your parents. They'll drive to the stables to pick you up."

"I can't leave!" Krista pleaded. "Comanche might turn around and come back to find me. What will he do if I'm not here?"

"He'll go home in the end," Richard insisted. He was calm and reassuring.

Krista shook her head. "But what if he's bleeding too badly to make it?"

"I've got my orders to take you back to

29

the stables," the man insisted. He opened the passenger door and waited for her to get into the car. "Jo seemed sure the pony would make its own way home."

Sighing and shaking her head, Krista did as she was told. "I can't believe what happened!" she groaned, re-running in her mind the moment when the Land Rover had first appeared round the bend. It seemed to go in

slow motion – the rattle of the trailer, the moment of total fear as Krista realized it was going to crash into them. Now, as she sat in the soft leather seat, she felt herself begin to tremble and her head spun.

Richard eased his car forward until he came to a gateway where he did a three-point turn to face the way they'd come. "Everything will be fine," he promised, driving back up the winding hill.

But Krista looked over her shoulder at the spot where the accident had happened. She was in time to see the last rays of sun shining over the horizon. The sky was aglow with burning light, but the fields were empty, and of poor, injured Comanche there was no sign.

Chapter Three

"Now, tell me everything – exactly as it happened!" Jo greeted Krista in the stable yard with a hug and a big box of tissues. She thanked Richard Bradley, who was now in a hurry to be on his way.

"Glad I could help," he said with a kindly pat of Krista's shoulder before he left. "And I hope everything turns out fine."

Krista sighed then blew her nose, anxious to tell Jo everything she could. "It was a Land Rover with a woman driver. I didn't have time to get the registration number."

Red Skies

Jo led her into the house, where her two black cats stood at the door miaowing for their supper. "And she didn't stop?" Jo asked.

Krista shook her head. She was still shaking from shock, holding her shoulder which was beginning to hurt badly. "She drove on without checking we were OK — which we weren't!"

"Hit and run," Jo muttered with a frown. "I hate that!"

"I wish I knew who it was."

"Never mind. For the moment, our priority is to get a doctor to look at your shoulder. Also, your ankle. It looks like you're limping."

"I'm fine, honest. Maybe a bruise or a sprain, that's all."

My Magical Pony

Sitting her down in the living room, Jo paced up and down. "Your mum should be here any minute. She'll probably want the doctor to check you over."

Krista took a deep, stuttering breath. "It's Comanche I'm worried about," she confessed. "The trailer swung into him and knocked him over. When he got up again there was a cut this big across his nose!" She held up two shaking fingers to show Jo, who nodded thoughtfully.

"Which way did he run?" she asked.

"I tried to catch hold of him!" Krista gabbled, screwing up her face and keeping her eyes shut. "He reared up and got away. Then he jumped the wall and ran up the hill."

34

"Towards home?"

Krista nodded. "I expected him to be here by now."

"Not yet," Jo said slowly. She came to a halt at the bay window and looked out across the sloping fields where other ponies grazed. The light had almost faded from the sky, lending a ghostly grey air to the hillside.

My Magical Pony

"It'll be dark soon," Krista sighed. Desperate to see Comanche trotting up the hill, she went to join Jo at the window.

I know who I need to talk to! she thought. This was something she couldn't say out loud. Her magical pony, Shining Star, was a secret she didn't share with anyone. She'd made him a promise that she would never, never break. *If ever I needed his help, it's now!* she thought.

"Here's your mum." Jo pointed out the car driving in from the lane. She went out quickly and began to explain what had happened.

Krista's mum soon rushed into the house. "Are you—?"

"—I'm fine!" Krista cut in. "I didn't break anything – look!"

Red Skies

"You're limping!" her mum cried as Krista walked towards her. "I need to take you to hospital."

"No. Really, Mum, I'm OK. Did you see Comanche in the lane?"

"No, there's no sign of him. But I sent your dad out looking for him. And I stopped in town and told John Carter what had happened. He said that Jo should give him a call as soon as Comanche shows up."

"See, everything's under control." Jo stepped up to reassure Krista. "The vet will be here to put stitches in the wound. He'll give old Commy a shot of antibiotics and he'll be as right as rain."

Krista wanted to believe what she was

37

hearing, but a major worry niggled at her. "Where is he now?" she asked. "If he headed for home across the fields, he should have beaten us!"

"He'll be here," Jo insisted steadily. She put her arm around Krista to lead her to her mum's car.

"Ouch!" Krista winced as Jo's hand rested on her shoulder.

"You need to see a doctor!" Krista's mum said firmly.

"And I need to get out there and have a scout around for

Comanche," Jo added. "Bye, Krista. I'll ring as soon as I have any news."

Reluctantly Krista got into the car. "Jo, I'm so sorry," she began. "I wish I hadn't decided to come home on the road …"

But Jo shook her head. "Definitely not your fault."

"But …" Krista's head was full of "if onlys". *If only I hadn't stopped to talk to those two kids. If only we'd headed straight home!*

"No, Krista, you have to believe it," Jo insisted. "No way is this down to you. Richard Bradley swears that the woman was breaking the speed limit."

"Let's get you home," Krista's mum said finally. "You need a good night's sleep,

then I'll take you into the surgery first thing tomorrow morning to get checked out."

I need to get to the magic spot! Krista thought as her mum drove her home. The sky was dark, there was a pale new moon overhead. *Shining Star will help us find Comanche, even in the dark!*

"Your dad and I were worried out of our minds when we got the news," her mum said quietly. She drove carefully along the lanes. "Your dad immediately thought the worst. He was ready to dash to the hospital."

"Sorry," Krista sighed. "But Comanche and me – we were having a cool time until it happened. I still can't believe it."

"I know one thing for sure – your dad

would wring that driver's neck if he could
get his hands on her. Me too." Krista's mum
thought out loud, while Krista kept her secret
thoughts to herself.

My Magical Pony

Shining Star, please come! It's urgent. I need you!
As they approached the stile leading to the
cliff path and the magic spot, Krista wondered
how she could get her mum to stop the car. *I
only need a couple of minutes to call him*, she thought.
*He's magic — he can hear me from miles and miles away.
Then he would fly from Galishe and be here at the click
of my fingers. If only I could reach the magic spot!*

But there was no excuse she could think of
that would make her mum stop the car in the
dark. Instead she sat in silence as they passed
the stile in the lane.

"Hot chocolate and bed!" her mum declared,
turning into the yard at High Point Farm.

"Did you feed Spike for me?" Krista
remembered as she got out of the car.

42

Red Skies

"Yes, don't worry, he's been fed and watered!" Ushering her into the house, Krista's mum heaved a sigh of relief. "We're home!" she called to Krista's dad, who appeared at the top of the stairs.

"I ran a nice hot bath," he told Krista with an anxious glance at her pale face. "And your pyjamas are warming on the radiator in the bathroom."

Krista nodded and trudged upstairs.

"You're limping!" he declared.

"It's nothing," she sighed. *Please come!* she called silently to Shining Star. *Comanche needs you. I need you!*

There was no reply. Slowly Krista went into the bathroom and closed the door.

Chapter Four

"Of course, that's only to be expected." First thing next morning the doctor in the GP's surgery examined Krista's ankle and listened to her mum's explanation of what had happened. "Krista would be too shocked to get much sleep. I'm not surprised she lay awake most of the night."

Talk to me as if I'm here! Krista thought with a frown. Her ankle had swollen and her shoulder still hurt.

"This ankle is sprained but I'm pretty sure it's not broken," the doctor told her mum.

Red Skies

"We'll strap it up with a strong elastic bandage."

"What about the shoulder?" Krista's mum asked.

Krista stared around the room at the eye-test chart on the wall and the computer screen on the desk. *OK, so go ahead and talk about me!*

"The same with the shoulder. It's not actually dislocated, but she should rest it as much as possible." The young woman doctor sat at her desk and typed at her keyboard. "She can have a few days off school if she wants."

Quickly Krista jumped in. "No thanks!" She'd rather keep busy than be hanging around at home, where her mum would keep an eagle eye on her. She formed a plan to go on as normal, and when she was on her way home

that night she would seize her chance to slip along the cliff path to the magic spot. "I've got a daughter who goes horse riding," the doctor told them. "I know how upsetting the accident must have been. But I take it the pony made his way home OK?"

Krista's mum shook her head. "Not yet. Jo Weston, the owner, rang us first thing this morning. Comanche still hasn't shown up."

Krista swallowed hard then gritted her teeth. The news had come as a fresh blow and made her feel like bursting into tears every time she was reminded of it.

"Hmm." The doctor frowned. "That's strange."

"Of course, Jo and a couple of friends are out looking again."

Red Skies

"I wanted to go with them." For the first time Krista spoke up. "Mum wouldn"t let me."

"You heard what the doctor said – you need to take it easy," her mum argued. "No way am I letting you roam across the moors looking for a lost pony!"

"Quite right." The doctor took sides with her mum. "And if you do go to school, make sure you don't overdo things."

Sighing, Krista had to agree. But she was silent as she and her mum left the surgery and drove to school.

It was playtime when they arrived and kids were out in the playground.

Frowning, Krista got out of the car and hobbled through the gates.

"Follow doctor's orders – take it easy!" her mum called after her. "I'll pick you up after school!"

Oh no! What about Shining Star? I won't be able to slip away to the magic spot! But Krista knew there was no point arguing, so she nodded and limped on.

"Hey, what happened to you?" Janey Bellwood cried, running up to Krista, with Alice Henderson close on her heels.

"I had an accident," Krista mumbled. Soon she was surrounded by friends, forced to tell every detail of what had happened.

It was the longest day of Krista's life.

Red Skies

She sat through each lesson without listening, just staring out of the window, thinking about the missing pony. The hours crawled by, but at last the bell rang for the end of school.

"Krista, over here!" her mum called from the gate. She'd been waiting anxiously to see whether Krista was all right.

Slowly Krista limped across. "Any news?" she asked.

Her mum shook her head. "Jo's still out looking."

"Oh Mum, something really bad has happened!" Krista groaned, sinking into the car seat. "I can't bear it!"

"It's not looking good," her mum admitted

as she drove home. "But we have to think positive – there's still a chance that Comanche will turn up."

"How? When?" It was nearly twenty-four hours since the accident and Krista's hopes had drained away. Now she felt wretched and empty, as if the bottom had dropped out of her world. She sat in a daze, not even noticing when her mum pulled into the yard at High Point.

"Come on, love, we're home," her mum said gently.

Once inside the house, Krista went straight up to her room. She gazed out of the window, across the yard towards the moors. "Shining Star, I need you!" she whispered.

Red Skies

"Can you hear me?"

For a while she waited, picturing her magical pony flying over the horizon and soaring down the hill towards her. She saw fluffy white clouds and imagined that it was him surrounded by his silvery mist. But when she waited for his shape to emerge she was disappointed and her heart sank further still.

Then Krista's thoughts turned back to the mystery of the missing pony. "Comanche,

where are you?" she murmured, as if speaking
his name would bring him back.

Her mum called her downstairs for tea.
"You must eat something," she insisted when
Krista said once more that she wasn't hungry.

So Krista tried a couple of mouthfuls,
fiddling with pasta on the plate. Then suddenly
she thought of an excuse to escape. "Mum, I
just remembered – I haven't fed Spike."

"Sit. Eat," her mum insisted.

"Can I go outside when I've finished?"

Her mum nodded. "Just into the garden."

Forcing the food down, Krista took a
gulp of orange juice then excused herself.
She poured milk into Spike's saucer and
scooped cat food from a tin. "Won't be long,"

she said as she limped out into the garden.

As soon as she was in the fresh air, she felt somehow more hopeful. "Here, Spike!" she called softly.

The little hedgehog came running from under the hedge at the bottom of the garden. Quickly he attacked the dish of food.

"Greedy!" Krista murmured, almost smiling. She looked up at the hillside. *Maybe ... But Mum said to stay here,* she reminded herself. She snuck a look at the house. *Maybe she wouldn't miss me if I slipped out for a few minutes ...*

"Krista?" a voice called.

"Still here," she replied.

"Listen, love, I've run a bath. I'm going to have a quiet soak. Will you be OK?"

53

My Magical Pony

"Fine!" Taking another deep breath, Krista gathered her courage. "I'll stay out here with Spike!"

The back door closed and she waited for three minutes, counting them on her watch. *OK, Mum must be in the bath by now – this is my chance!*

As Spike gobbled greedily, Krista slipped off. She crossed the lane and made for the stile, climbing it awkwardly with her bandaged leg. The magic spot was within sight – about two hundred metres along the cliff path.

"Hurry!" Krista muttered to herself. She felt the wind gather strength as it blew off the sea and saw the sun peep out from behind golden clouds that had gathered on the horizon.

Red Skies

Way below, the glittering sea broke and crashed over dark rocks.

She counted the steps until she came to the secret place – a hundred, a hundred and thirty, a hundred and eighty. She was almost there, close enough to the tall rock that marked the spot to see the tiny purple flowers growing in clusters at its base. "Shining Star!" she called in a loud voice, cupping her hands around her mouth so that her voice would carry. "It's me, Krista! Something terrible has happened. Please come!"

More clouds gathered over the sea. The wind blew them towards the shore.

"Comanche is missing!" Krista called, turning to face the looming hillside.

55

The magical pony might come from any direction – north, south, east or west. "He's hurt. Shining Star, I'm scared!"

The sky above the rocky horizon was clear. A grey bird swooped towards her, giving a loud, high screech.

"Please come!" Krista called, turning again.

Red Skies

Now the clouds had reached the curve of the bay. The beach darkened. In the midst of the shadows a silver light gleamed.

"Shining Star!" Krista whispered. She held her breath and waited.

"Krista, I hear you," a voice said, drifting on the wind.

She looked for the telltale mist of silver dust drifting to the ground. Soon the magical pony would appear, his beautiful neck arched, his white wings spread wide. "Where are you?"

"I cannot come at this moment," Star replied. "I have a task to complete which is far away from your world. But speak and I will hear."

"We've lost Comanche," Krista gasped. "He was hurt in an accident. Shining Star, I'm scared!"

"I know the pony you speak about," the voice of Shining Star said. "He is wise and loyal."

"He's the best!" Krista agreed. "There isn't a pony at Hartfell who you can trust more than you can trust Comanche. That's why he wouldn't stay away if he could help it."

There was silence then Star spoke again. "I believe you are right," he agreed softly. "But there are many reasons why he may not return."

"Such as?" Krista cried. She could only think that poor Comanche had bled so much

58

that he was too weak to move.

"Perhaps he has taken shelter until his wound heals," Star said after another long gap. "It is natural for a horse to do so. Or perhaps someone has taken him in and is caring for him."

Krista nodded. "Yes. I didn't think of that. But in that case, why haven't we heard any news?"

"I don't know," the magical pony said, his voice growing fainter as the wind grew stronger and the evening clouds cast a cold shadow over Krista. "But listen, I have heard your call and I will come as soon as I can."

"When will that be?" she pleaded.

"Tomorrow," Shining Star promised.

"But I must go now."

"In the morning?" she cried, feeling afraid as her magical pony's voice faded. What would she do without him? How could she possibly wait?

"Tomorrow," his voice said again. It seemed to give off a faint echo before it fell silent.

"Come as soon as you can," she whispered, turning from the spot and limping slowly back home.

Chapter Five

"'Red sky at night, shepherd's delight,'" Krista recalled. "'Red sky in the morning, shepherd's warning!'"

She'd woken at dawn and rushed to the window. The sky was ablaze with red light.

Oh no, that's not good! she thought. A red sky now must mean something else bad was about to happen.

Krista stared out across the garden, beyond the lane, towards the magic spot. She wondered if she had time to slip away before her mum and dad woke up, but when she

tried to put her full weight on her swollen ankle she winced and realized that she wouldn't be able to run there and back in time.

Should I risk it? she wondered. *Shining Star said he would come when he could. Perhaps it's now!*

Her bedroom door clicked open. "Awake already?" her dad said.

Too late! "I couldn't sleep," she admitted with a sigh.

"Me neither. Come on downstairs. Let's make breakfast." He waited for her and they went down together. "I thought I'd give Jo a ring soon," her dad went on, switching on the kettle and popping bread in the toaster. "It's a bit early right now, but if we wait thirty minutes or so, we should catch her

before she sets off on another search."

"She'd have rung us if there was any news," Krista mumbled. Now that Comanche had been missing for two nights, she knew that Jo's chances of finding him were slim. "Hey, I wonder if she's been back to the place where we had the accident and tried to pick up his trail?"

"Good thinking," her dad agreed.

"Can I ring her now and ask her?" Krista asked, jumping up from her chair. She felt so useless doing nothing, just sitting there.

"OK, go ahead. I don't suppose anyone's getting much sleep right now."

So Krista called Jo's number, and sure enough Jo was already up. "Yes, I did go back to the lane," she replied in answer to

Krista's eager question. "It was on the bend just past the Dudley place, wasn't it?"

Ben and Trevor Dudley were brothers who ran a sheep farm on the fields running up towards the moor. "That's right," Krista said.

"I called there yesterday afternoon," Jo told her. "You know what Trevor and Ben are like – they didn't say much! But it seems that they were out at the time, so they hadn't a clue what had happened, though Trevor did notice broken glass in the road."

"But did you search in the field for Comanche's hoof prints? Maybe he left tracks."

"Wouldn't that be handy?" Jo sighed. "Then we could just use our old girl guide tracking skills to follow his trail. But no – no such luck."

Red Skies

Krista frowned and fell silent.

"I'll take another look if you like," Jo offered.

"Maybe I should come too!"

Krista's dad quickly shook his head. "You're going to school," he insisted.

"But Dad, I'm the only one who knows exactly where Comanche jumped the wall and took off up the hill!"

"School!" he insisted.

My Magical Pony

"I heard what your dad said," Jo cut in.
"And I agree. You have to stick to routine,
Krista, and try not to worry."

"Like – how?" These grown-ups might just
as well say "try not to breathe"!

"I know, it's hard. But go to school and
then this evening maybe your mum or your
dad could drive you to Hartfell and I'll fill you
in on all the latest developments."

"OK." Krista gave in and handed the
phone back to her dad. As he talked on, she
wandered outside, shaking her head.

By now the red dawn had faded and the
sky was a calm, pale blue. Krista drew a
deep breath and gazed into the distance.
There was a bright light over the moor,

growing stronger and coming towards her.

What's that? Krista gasped. She looked harder and listened.

"Krista, come to the magic spot!" Shining Star said. His voice surrounded her, the silver light shone on the hillside.

"I'm on my way!" she told him, forgetting all thoughts of following doctor's orders. She wasn't due at school for hours! Instead, she half ran, half limped into the lane, her eyes fixed on the shining light. She climbed the stile and rushed on.

Over the magic spot Shining Star scattered his silver dust. He soared down from the horizon in a glittering cloud, hovering in the air, waiting for Krista.

My Magical Pony

She heard the sound of his wings beating and felt a rush of warm air surround her as she approached the spot. "Shining Star, I knew you'd come!" she said, closing her eyes for a moment, knowing that when she opened them her magical pony would be gazing down on her.

He came with a blaze of silver light, appearing out of the glittering mist. He looked down and saw Krista – a small, dark-haired figure looking up at him with troubled eyes.

"Do not be afraid," he said.

"I'm not – now that you're here," she murmured, waiting for him to land.

Star folded his broad wings and shook glittering dust across the ground. He tossed his white mane back from his face, noticing the bandage around her ankle. "You are hurt."

"Not much. Not like Comanche."

"No need to explain," he decided. "I can sense that the piebald pony is unable to return, though he longs to be back with those who care for him."

"He's alive!" Krista gasped. She knew of old the magical pony's power to see what others could not.

"Alive but trapped," Star confirmed.

"Something prevents him from going home, but I cannot make out what it is."

"Can you see where he is?" Krista urged, reaching out a hand to steady herself against Shining Star. A warm wind still blew around them, causing the mist to whirl and sparkle.

"A place where there is food and water, but no other ponies," the magical pony replied. He seemed to be listening and looking intently. Then he turned his head to Krista. "It is our job to find him."

"Yes!" she cried. What she loved about Star was that he was strong and determined, even when hope had sunk so low.

His dark eyes gazed into hers. "Then climb on my back," he ordered. "Fly with me."

Chapter Six

There was always this moment with Shining Star when he spread his wings and the magic happened.

Krista sat astride his broad back and clung to his mane. She felt his strong wings lift them from the ground and held her breath.

They rose high above the moor. To one side the wide arc of Whitton Bay stretched towards Black Point. To the other, the moors rose and rolled as far as she could see.

"Hold tight," Star told her. "Be ready to fly back through the night which has just passed,

and through the day and night before that."

Krista nodded. She crouched low over his smooth white neck. Shining Star was wonderful. Now that he was here, her hopes rose. "You're taking us back to Sunday!" she murmured.

"We will start where it began," he confirmed. "Are you ready?"

She clutched his mane with both hands. They rose high above the bay into the pale blue sky, gathering silver clouds around them. The clouds carried them swiftly, hiding the sands and the glittering sea. They wrapped themselves around Shining Star and Krista, forming a shining tunnel which took them back through time. The tunnel whirled,

Red Skies

sparks of silver flew around their heads like shooting stars.

They came through the darkness into bright light. Krista felt the heat of the sun beyond the tunnel of whirling clouds. It glowed golden and warmed her face as Shining Star's wings beat rapidly and carried them on, back into darkness and between yet more silver stars. They passed through a second night. Krista saw the moon shining at the end of the dark passage. Then it faded against a clear blue sky, which was their magical journey's end.

Shining Star flew out into the sunny day. Krista looked down on Whitton Bay and saw two boys building sandcastles.

It took a few seconds for Krista to realize

when she had first seen the boys.

"Comanche and I walked past them up the beach towards the town," she told Shining Star. "I didn't want to gallop him back along the beach."

She felt her heart beat faster as she rode Shining Star along the road where the accident had happened. Memories flooded back of sturdy Comanche stepping out willingly even though he was tired, of the sudden roar of a car engine and the shock when Krista had seen the Land Rover speeding towards them. For a few terrible moments she was afraid they were going to re-live the accident over again and that she was about to see herself and Comanche come to grief.

My Magical Pony

But when Star came to the bend, she studied the ground and saw pieces of shattered glass glinting up at her. "It's already happened!" she murmured.

"Not long ago," Shining Star confirmed. He looked around, taking in the sharp bend and the high walls. "This is a dangerous place," he added quietly.

"And there's a car coming right now!" Krista warned, so that Star could quickly beat his wings and fly just high enough to clear the wall and land in the field alongside. "It's OK – I think it's going to stop," she added.

Sure enough an old red car rattled into view. The driver braked then stopped. A man got out of the passenger side.

Red Skies

"What's happened here?" he grumbled.

Krista peered over the wall and watched him kick some of the splintered glass to the side of the road.

The driver, who had the same bald head and long thin face as his passenger, leaned out of the window. "Another crash," he muttered. "I expect the idiot took the bend too wide."

"You bet she did!" Krista said, suddenly climbing the wall and perching on top.

"She was going way too fast!"

"Whoa, were did you pop up from?" the driver asked, stepping out of the car. "And what's it got to do with you?"

"It was me she nearly hit!" Krista exclaimed. She took care to keep her bandaged ankle hidden.

"Hey, Trevor, come here," the man said. "This lass has had a nasty shock."

The two Dudley brothers took a good look at Krista then glanced over the wall at Shining Star. Because of the magical pony's powers, all they saw was a little moorland pony with a shaggy mane hanging over his face.

Star snickered and bent his head to graze,

as if Krista and the men were none of
his business.

"Was this the pony?" Ben Dudley asked,
perhaps wondering if Krista had caught a
wild pony and been riding him bareback.
The old farmer seemed ready to give her a
good telling-off.

She shook her head. "No, this is a different
one. Mine is a piebald. He's called Comanche.
Did you see him?"

Both men leaned on the wall and shook
their heads.

"Accidents are always happening on this
bend," Trevor muttered. "It's a miracle no one's
been killed."

"Yet!" Ben added gloomily.

My Magical Pony

"So you didn't see a Land Rover and trailer speeding off?" Krista checked.

"I haven't seen anyone on the road since we came out of Maythorne," Ben insisted. "Oh, hang on a sec – I did catch sight of Richard Bradley's little sportscar in the distance."

Krista's eyes widened. "Oh no, that was—" She stopped herself just in time from spilling out the fact that Richard Bradley had been the person who'd rescued her and taken her back to Hartfell. "I mean, that wasn't the car that almost crashed into us. It was a dark green Land Rover pulling a silver trailer."

Ben Dudley shook his head and checked out Shining Star for a second time.

Red Skies

But his brother scratched his head and came out with a different answer. "You know, come to think of it, I did catch a glimpse of a Land Rover and trailer heading up the side lane towards the moor top."

"You did?" In her excitement Krista jumped down from the wall and landed on her sore ankle. "Ouch! Did you recognize it? Do you know whose it was?"

Trevor frowned. "I'm not sure. If it was who I was thinking of, it definitely wasn't heading for home, because that would be along this road, back towards Maythorne."

Krista was eager to hear more, but his grumpier brother cut in. "Hang on, Trevor, are you sure about this?"

"Yes, I tell you, I did see a trailer," Trevor insisted. "It was brand new. That's why I clocked it from a distance. I was thinking, 'That must be Clive Barnes's trailer.' He's the only one round here with enough cash to throw around on stuff like that."

"Clive Barnes!" Krista repeated the name.

Trevor Dudley nodded. "I'm not saying it was him for sure. In fact, it's more likely it was his daughter, Alexa. She's the one who drives down these lanes like a maniac."

"Alexa Barnes," Krista whispered. Now she was sure she was on to something. The first piece of the jigsaw was slotting into place. "Can you tell me where she lives?"

"I'm still not sure you should be telling her

82

this," Ben muttered, retreating to his car and impatiently calling his brother after him.

"Please!" Krista begged.

Trevor Dudley gave his head one last scratch. "The Barneses live at Little Lane Farm just outside Maythorne," he told her. "Go and take a look. But whatever you do, don't tell them I sent you!"

Chapter Seven

As soon as the two farmers had driven on, Krista climbed the wall and hurried back to Shining Star. "I've found out the name of the woman who was driving the Land Rover!" she gabbled. "She's called Alexa Barnes and—"

"I heard what the man said," Star interrupted. "We will go to her house and see what we can find out."

Quickly Krista scrambled on to his back. "If I see her and find out she really was the woman driving that Land Rover, I'll …" Stuck for words, Krista held tight as the

magical pony spread his wings. "... Well, I don't know what I'll do!"

"Do not be angry," Star advised. "Our task is to find out more. Anger will get in the way."

"I'll try," Krista promised with a frown. She felt the earth slip away below them as they rose into the sky and flew over the fields. Soon the sheep and lambs became tiny grey and white dots on a vast green background.

"Perhaps Alexa saw where Comanche ran to," Star reminded her. "You say you saw him galloping up the hill?"

"That was the last I saw of him," she agreed.

"And Trevor glimpsed the Land Rover and trailer driving towards the top of the moor, remember."

"Yes." Suddenly Krista saw what Star was getting at. "Maybe Alexa will have more news about where he was headed!"

"Let's find out." Flying towards the sea where the sun was sinking in the west, Shining Star spread his wings and floated on warm air currents. He scanned the coastline, picking out clusters of small houses lining the shore. "Which one is Maythorne?" he asked.

Krista shielded her eyes against the low rays of the sun. It was strange to look down on a miniature world that she knew so well, but she soon pointed to a village. "I think that's it."

Shining Star swerved towards it and gathered speed. "Little Lane Farm," he

86

murmured, swooping over rocky inlets. "Let us find the place where Alexa lives."

With the wind in her hair, Krista concentrated on the search. They passed over a row of small houses built around a narrow harbour with a stone jetty like a crooked finger pointing out to sea.

"This is definitely the right village," she told Star. "Little Lane Farm must be somewhere near here."

My Magical Pony

Slowly Star circled the area. They saw a farm nestled against the hill and flew low over it. Krista read the name on the gatepost – "Huby Farm". "That's not it," she sighed.

The magical pony flew on, keeping low. He spotted a narrow winding lane leading up to an isolated farmhouse and once more he hovered. "Little Lane Farm!" Krista read. "At last!"

So Shining Star landed gently at the end of the lane and they began the long walk towards the house.

"Gosh, I'm scared!" Krista murmured as they drew near. "I don't know what to expect."

"Stay calm," Star insisted. As they reached the farmyard to the side of the house, he stopped. "I will wait here. Find out all you can."

88

Red Skies

Taking a deep breath, Krista went on alone. She saw that the yard was neat and tidy. There was a tractor parked by a wall, next to a tall barn. Beyond that was a row of stables. *Hmm, they keep horses,* she thought, and headed towards the stables. Inside the first she found a beautiful dark bay mare nursing a tiny chestnut foal.

Krista's heart melted at the sight of the baby suckling from its mother. The mare looked up and gave a warning snicker.

"It's OK, I'm not going to disturb you," Krista whispered as she tiptoed on. She glanced over her shoulder and saw Shining Star waiting outside the yard. Then she went to the barn and peered inside.

My Magical Pony

It was stacked high with bales of hay and straw. A ginger cat nestled in a corner.

"Nothing much here!" Krista murmured, turning back again.

It was then that she heard voices coming from behind the barn – a man and a young woman were arguing.

"Look at the state of this!" the man said angrily. "I can't even trust you to drive into

town without scraping or smashing something!"

"You're always blaming me for stuff I didn't do!" the woman retorted. "This light was broken before I took the car out!"

Krista clenched her fists. *Yes!* She crept to the corner of the barn and peered down the side. Sure enough, there was the Land Rover and silver trailer that had crashed into Comanche. Beside it stood a tall, middle-aged man and a very young, blonde-haired woman dressed in sweatshirt and jeans – Clive and Alexa Barnes!

"You're talking rubbish!" Clive raised his voice. "There was nothing wrong with this Land Rover when I drove it earlier today. Now look – the light's smashed, and there's a dent

half a mile deep in the side of the trailer!"

"You always make things worse than they are," Alexa argued back. "The dent's tiny. Nobody will notice."

"And you still say it wasn't you?" By now Clive Barnes sounded furious. "A brand new trailer with a dirty great dent, and it's not your fault!"

"OK, well listen, maybe something happened while I was parked by the harbour." Swiftly changing tack, Alexa made up another excuse. "You know how crowded it is in Maythorne on a Sunday. I bet some nitwit bumped into my car while I was in the café dropping off something for Lee's mum. They must've driven off without owning up."

Red Skies

Fibber! Krista watched as Alexa's father considered this. Clive Barnes had bent down to inspect the broken headlight. When he stood up, he shook his head and roughly took Alexa by the arm. "I'll let you off for now," he told her nastily. "But if I find out you're lying, I'll ban you from driving any vehicle belonging to me. You'll never get behind the wheel again. Is that clear?"

Alexa backed off and nodded. "It's the truth, Dad – honest!" She was desperate to get away, and in her haste she pulled her arm free.

Clive Barnes overbalanced and fell against the Land Rover. As he got up, he spotted Krista out of the corner of his eye. "Hey you!" he yelled.

My Magical Pony

Krista jumped back out of sight. She heard footsteps running towards her and set off across the yard. But she couldn't run fast because of her ankle. Soon the angry farmer caught her up.

"What are you doing snooping around here?" he demanded, planting himself in front of Krista, hands on hips. He was wide as well as tall, with broad shoulders and strong arms. He'd looked around and already taken in the little grey moorland pony waiting at the gate.

"I'm ... I wasn't ..." Krista stammered. She was on the point of blurting out the truth about his daughter and her bad driving, when Star raised his head and whinnied. *Keep calm!*

she reminded herself. *We have to find out more about Comanche.* "Sorry," she muttered, ready to beat a retreat.

"Are you lost, or what?" Clive Barnes demanded, taken aback by the apology.

Quickly Krista nodded.

"There's no bridleway through here. Take your pony back along the lane and turn left. You'll see the signpost. Now get on your way!" Turning on his heel, the farmer strode away.

"Phew!" Krista rolled her eyes. "Scary man!"

Shining Star agreed. "His daughter is afraid of him too."

"Yeah, too scared to admit the truth about the accident. Come on, Star, I think we'd better do as he says."

"The daughter is afraid of her father's anger about the car and of something else too," the magical pony insisted. He stayed at the gate as Krista set off down the lane.

Krista turned to wait for him. The last rays of sunlight had faded. Darkness was settling on Little Lane Farm. "Maybe. But we're no nearer to finding Comanche, are we?"

"Ah, but we are," Shining Star said, looking deep into her eyes. "Krista, we are much closer than you think."

Chapter Eight

So, what big secret is Alexa keeping? Krista asked herself. *And how can we find out?*

She and Shining Star stood in the dusk light at the end of the rough lane. Not far away, waves crashed against the pebble beach. A pale silver moon appeared in the sky.

"We will stay here," Shining Star decided. He glanced at Krista, who drew breath and shivered. "The night grows cold. Stand close and keep warm."

Gratefully Krista put her arms around the magical pony's neck. "Are we keeping watch?"

My Magical Pony

Star nodded. "We must speak to Alexa when she is alone. The key to this mystery lies with her."

"It's weird. When I first saw her I expected to feel really angry, but I didn't," Krista confessed. "Actually, I felt a bit sorry for her."

"Who knows why she drove too fast, or why she sped away from the accident?" Star asked.

Krista thought this through. "Maybe there was a reason we don't know about."

"In any case, you must talk to her." Determined as ever, Shining Star set off in the dim light across a field where two horses grazed. Krista followed.

Briefly the horses raised their heads.

Red Skies

They twitched their ears and flared their nostrils then went back to feeding.

"Where are we going now?" she asked.

"Back to the house by a different path," the magical pony explained. "The girl's father must not see us. We will lie low and hope that she appears."

"There's another weird thing," Krista said as they crept closer to the house. "I never expected Alexa Jennings to be into horses from the way she acted when she crashed into us – like she couldn't care less. But she's got these two in the field, plus the gorgeous mare and foal in the stable."

"Ah, a mare and foal," Star repeated softly.

"Yeah, so sweet and tiny!"

My Magical Pony

"Hush!" Shining Star warned as a light came on in the front porch. They waited quietly in the shadow of a tree, but no one came out of the house.

Darkness settled on the hillside. Stars appeared. A cold wind blew.

"Lights are going off in the downstairs rooms," Krista whispered. "It looks like Alexa's not coming out."

"Wait!" was her magical pony's reply.

Then at last, the front door opened and Alexa came into the garden.

Krista darted behind the tree until the sound of Alexa's voice drew her forward. She glanced at the magical pony.

"Yes, go," Shining Star urged. "But take care."

Red Skies

Krista crouched low and crept towards the garden.

"Lee, it's me." Alexa Barnes spoke quietly into her cell phone. "Yeah, I'm OK. Dad was furious about the headlight, but I managed to fob him off with an excuse."

As silently as she could, Krista followed Alexa round the front of the house into the yard. Luckily Alexa was too busy talking to notice anything.

"Lee, listen. I'm really worried. I didn't manage to contact the vet about Dolly …

and no, I didn't get any antibiotics for – you know who … yes, that's what I'm saying, we still need the vet's advice."

There was a long pause as Alexa listened. "So you'll do it first thing in the morning? And you're sure he's OK?" she asked. "You've just been up there? Yeah, that sounds good."

Carefully Krista listened to every word, trying to make sense of what was being said. Without realizing it, she found she had followed Alexa into the barn.

"I wish I could press the rewind button," Alexa declared with a loud sigh. She paced up and down between the bales of straw. "I wouldn't have driven that fast if I'd known what was round the corner! … Yeah, Dad's

threatening to ban me from driving … Think what a disaster that would be!" After another long pause, she spoke again. But this time her voice was unsteady, as if she was beginning to cry. "Oh Lee, I've been so stupid! Yes, I know. But you being kind to me makes it worse."

Quickly Krista squeezed behind a stack of bales as Alexa wiped her eyes and turned to walk towards her.

Just then a shadow appeared in the doorway. The figure made Alexa jump. "Got to go!" she whispered hastily to Lee.

"I wondered where you were. Why tears?" Clive Barnes asked suspiciously.

Alexa sniffed and tried to look him in the eye. "Nothing. I'm OK."

"You're not fine. You're a wreck," Clive scoffed. "Don't tell me, you've been having another row with your precious boyfriend!"

"That's right!" Alexa came in too quickly with her admission.

"I don't know what you see in him anyway," Clive sneered. "Lee Harrison isn't nearly good enough for you, Alexa."

"Anyway, I really came out to check on Dolly and the new foal." Quickly Alexa changed the subject, pushing past her father and heading for the stables.

Clive Barnes followed and Krista saw that there was now no chance of getting Alexa to herself. It was no good – she would have to report back to her magical pony.

104

Red Skies

Slipping quietly out of the barn, Krista hurried to find Shining Star. She poured out the jumble of facts which she had just learned.

"Alexa's boyfriend is called Lee Harrison. She wants him to call the vet tomorrow morning. They need antibiotics. Maybe it's for the mare who's just given birth. Her name's Dolly.

Mr Barnes doesn't think Lee is good enough for Alexa …"

"Krista, slow down," Shining Star said. He'd listened thoughtfully but now wanted her to go back over something she'd said. "Are you sure that Alexa needs the vet for the mare in the barn? Could it be for someone else?"

Krista thought hard. "Well no, I'm not sure. In fact, it sounded as if there were two horses involved – Dolly and one whose name she wouldn't say."

"Think carefully," Star instructed. "Tell me exactly what she said."

Krista's frown deepened. "She said, 'I didn't get any antibiotics for – you know who.'"

106

Red Skies

Star nodded. "What else?"

"She asked Lee if he was sure 'he' was OK. Lee said he'd just been up there to check."

"Good," the magical pony said softly. "Well done, Krista."

Still puzzled, Krista spread her hands and shrugged. "What did I do?"

"You found out what we needed to know."

"I did?" Still she didn't see what Star was getting at.

"Climb on my back," he told her, ready to spread his wings and fly. "It is as I thought. Alexa is the one who rescued Comanche. She put him in the trailer and took him to her friend Lee's house. Now we must find out where he lives."

Chapter Nine

"I forgot to tell you – Lee's mother runs a café in Maythorne," Krista told Shining Star as they flew high in the night sky.

"Good. Now hold tight," he told her, flying faster, making the air whirl around them. "We will travel on through this night, into tomorrow and into a second darkness."

"You're taking us back to Tuesday!" a breathless Krista gasped. They soared into the dark tunnel that would take them through time.

"We know enough," he insisted. "We have discovered that Alexa has many troubles.

Red Skies

Now we must help her to unravel them."

Clinging on to his mane, Krista enjoyed the thrill of stars shooting over her head, trailing clouds of silver. She basked in the red light of dawn, seeing the sun's golden-red rays light up the clouds beneath their feet. The world appeared as a spinning mass of green and blue, then darkened for a second night, passing through glowing red to dull grey then deepest black and out into the red dawn of Tuesday.

"Wonderful!" she murmured as the dizzying journey came to an end.

Shining Star flew over Whitton Bay, slowly beating his broad wings. "Show me the café in Maythorne," he reminded her.

My Magical Pony

Krista directed him towards the tiny harbour and said he should land on the stone jetty next to the boats moored nearby. "It's still really early, so there won't be many people around. But why exactly have we come here?"

Once Star's feet had touched firm ground he folded his wings. "To seek out Lee Harrison's

mother. We must discover where he lives."

"OK, good plan!" Quickly dismounting, Krista sped off. She made for the cluster of houses at the harbour side, soon picking out the teashop sign swinging over one of the doors. She noticed a van parked outside and saw a man carrying a tray of fresh bread inside.

Krista hurried closer.

"Is that all for today?" the man was asking as he reappeared in the door.

"Yes thanks, Ken. I'll see you tomorrow," a woman's voice replied.

The delivery man slid his van door shut and drove off up the narrow street, leaving Krista to knock on the café door and enter.

My Magical Pony

"Hello!" she called, looking round the empty room.

There were tables with bright cloths, with matching curtains at the window. The smell of bread wafted towards Krista.

"You're too early. We're not open yet," a woman said, appearing from a room at the back. She was slight, with long dark hair pulled back from her face and held in a big pink butterfly clasp.

"I'm not a customer," Krista said hastily. "Actually, I'm looking for Lee."

"Uh-oh, what he done now?" Mrs Harrison asked. She didn't look worried as she set out knives and forks at each table. "He's always up to something."

Red Skies

"I just need to talk to him," Krista explained. "I thought you'd know where he was."

"Still in bed most likely. Oh no, come to think of it, he said he was going up to the barn first thing."

"The barn?"

"Yes. It's the old place he bought to do up. One of his crazy ideas," his mother grumbled good naturedly. "It's got no roof or windows, no electricity either. But that's our Lee for you!"

"So where is it exactly?" Krista asked. "I know it's up on the moor somewhere. I just don't know how to get to it."

Lee's mum glanced up at Krista and decided there was no reason not to give her the directions. After all, what trouble could a

113

young girl in crumpled sweatshirt and worn jeans cause? "Are you on foot?" she asked.

"No. I'm riding my pony."

"Good, because it's a fair way off. You follow the main road out of here towards Whitton then take a left up towards Arncliff. Lee's barn is almost at the top, just before you reach the Falls. You can just see it from the road."

"Cool, thanks!" Giving Mrs Harrison a broad smile, Krista turned to go.

"If you find him, remind him to pick up my order from the supermarket in Whitton!" Mrs Harrison called as Krista closed the door behind her.

*

Red Skies

"We're on our way, Comanche!" Krista murmured as Shining Star trotted swiftly up the hill. She could hardly wait to find the missing pony sheltering safely in Lee Harrison's ruined barn.

The sound of Star's hooves on the road broke the peaceful silence of the early morning. A few sheep grazing on the moor raised their heads.

"We're almost there!" Krista whispered. She looked out eagerly for the old barn which Mrs Harrison had described.

My Magical Pony

"One thing still puzzles me," Shining Star said. "What made Alexa hide Comanche away from view?"

"Yeah, and I wonder what she would've planned to do if we hadn't shown up." Not for a second did Krista doubt her magical pony's version of what had happened on the day of the accident. In fact she was already picturing the moment when she would step inside the barn, see Comanche and fling her arms around his neck.

"I see the barn!" Star said. His keen eyes had spotted a single-storey stone building perched on the hill top. There was no lane leading to it – only a track through the heather worn by broad tractor wheels.

Red Skies

"Yes, that must be it!" Krista felt Star break into a canter as he made for the ruined building. *Soon!* she said to herself. *Comanche, you'll soon be free!*

Shining Star sped towards the barn. There was a tall ladder against one of the walls, a concrete mixer churning slowly on the scrubland at the front – it was just as Mrs Harrison had said; her son was here fixing the place up.

They reached the ruin and Krista slipped from Star's back. She was only a few steps away from finding Comanche.

"Hello!" Krista called. "Is anyone there?"

The mixer churned wet concrete inside the metal drum. Nobody answered.

My Magical Pony

"Lee?" Krista shouted.

Still no reply.

"Go inside," Star urged. "But be careful."

Holding her breath, Krista stepped forward. She pushed open an ancient door swinging on its rusty hinges, heard the drip of a tap on to stone flags, saw straw laid thickly across the floor. "Comanche?" she whispered.

She glanced up at big holes in the roof. Some wooden beams had rotted and fallen on to the animal stalls below. Only one partition remained. Krista trod cautiously over the splintered wood to peer inside.

There was a bed of fresh straw, a bucket of water. There was even Comanche's saddle and bridle slung over the wooden partition – but

118

there was no Comanche!

Krista let her head
drop and sighed heavily.
"He's not here," she
called to Shining Star.

"Lee left in haste,"
Star said. "Perhaps he
saw us coming."

"But where would he
take Comanche?" Almost
in tears, Krista scanned

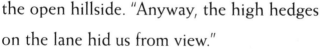

the open hillside. "Anyway, the high hedges
on the lane hid us from view."

"Then something else alarmed him," Star
decided. He pricked his ears and listened to
far-off sounds.

119

My Magical Pony

"At least we were right – Alexa did hide Comanche here. I saw his tack. And I guess he can't be far away."

"Listen!" Shining Star said. "A car is coming."

Sure enough, Krista soon glimpsed the flash of a car windscreen in the lane – someone was driving fast up the lane towards the barn. She and Shining Star retreated round the back of the barn, out of sight.

Alexa Barnes's Land Rover turned on to the rough track and rattled towards them. It stopped. A door slammed.

"Lee, where are you? It's me, Alexa!"

Krista heard footsteps hurry inside the barn then turn and come back out. She got ready to run.

Red Skies

"No, Krista. Stay here," Shining Star said.

"But …!" If Alexa discovered them and they challenged her face to face, she could deny everything. Then they would be as far away as ever from rescuing Comanche.

"Stay," Star insisted. He stood firm as Alexa approached.

"For heaven's sake, Lee, where are you? Where's the pony?" Alexa had searched the barn inside and out. She came around the corner, saw Krista and Star and stopped dead.

Krista drew a deep breath. She looked straight into the eyes of the woman who had hurtled round the bend and crashed into her beloved Comanche.

Chapter Ten

Alexa Barnes recognized Krista and backed away. She dropped her gaze and stumbled against the creaking barn door.

"How could you?" Krista began. Though Shining Star had warned her not to be angry with Alexa, she felt her blood boil. "What makes you drive like a maniac?" she demanded. "And where's Comanche? What have you done with him?"

"He should be here," Alexa stammered. "I don't know what's going on."

"So you admit you brought him here!"

Red Skies

"Yes, I did. Listen, I know the accident was my fault. I was in a mad hurry. My mare, Dolly, had mastitis and she was having trouble feeding her foal. I had to pick up a medicine from John Carter, the vet."

Krista took a deep breath. "Dolly was ill?"

Alexa nodded. "And the foal needed milk. He was getting weaker. I knew I had to act fast. But it's not an excuse for driving along the lane like that. Honestly, I'm really sorry for what I did!"

"Hmm." Krista paused for thought. She glanced at Shining Star who stood close by. "You almost killed us," she murmured.

"I know. And I drove on without stopping because all I could think of was getting the

medicine for Dolly." Alexa shook her head at the memory. "But then I came to my senses and decided I'd better turn around and face what I'd done. I reversed the trailer into a gateway and drove back along the lane, but by the time I reached the bend where it had happened, there was no one there."

"That's because another driver came along and helped me." Gradually Krista was beginning to calm down. "I'd hurt my ankle. He drove me back to Hartfell."

"I didn't realize that," Alexa murmured. She kept glancing anxiously down the hill. "I drove back and all I found was broken glass on the road. Then I looked across the field and there was the piebald pony, heading back."

Red Skies

"Comanche came back?" Krista faltered.

Alexa nodded. "His face was covered in blood and I could see he needed help. I didn't know who he belonged to or where he lived."

"So you grabbed him and put him in your trailer?" Krista prompted. "But why did you decide to hide him up here?"

"I was torn," Alexa admitted. "I knew he should see a vet, but I was scared of what my dad would say when he found out I'd caused an accident. You don't know what he's like ..." She paused and took another frightened glance towards the lane. "I get scared when he loses his temper."

At this, Shining Star stepped up beside Krista. He stretched his neck and nuzzled

Alexa's arm. She half smiled and stroked his nose. "Sweet!" she murmured.

He's more than sweet — he's good and brave and will help anyone in trouble, if only you knew! Krista thought.

"All I can say is that I was in a total panic," Alexa sighed. "I brought the piebald up here, called Lee and told him what I'd done then raced down to the vet's house. But by then

Red Skies

John Carter had left and so I didn't have any medicine either for Dolly or your little piebald. And then Dad rang to ask me where I was, saying I should've been home ages ago. I didn't have any choice – I had to drive back."

"But Lee did come up to check on Comanche soon after." Krista remembered the conversation she'd overheard at Little Lane Farm.

"Lee's amazing." Pacing up and down, Alexa wrung her hands. "He never lets me down. Dad had grounded me, but Lee brought hay and water for your pony and washed the blood from his face. Luckily the cut wasn't too deep and Lee said it would heal without stitches."

"So what then?" Now Krista understood the mess Alexa had got herself into.

My Magical Pony

"I don't know!" Alexa wailed. "I was still too scared to own up. But yesterday news got around the neighbourhood that the injured pony belonged to Jo Weston at Hartfell." She shook her head in desperation. "There was a search party out looking for him. That scared me even more. So I guess Lee and I were still trying to work out how to get him back home without being found out."

"But where is Comanche now?" Krista demanded, pointing to the empty stall. "I don't get it. What went wrong?"

This time there was a long pause before Alexa came out with the answer. Then she whispered, "Dad discovered what I'd done."

Krista took a step back. "How come?"

Red Skies

"He put two and two together – about the missing pony from Hartfell and the broken headlight and everything. First thing this morning he stormed into my room and put the pressure on, yelling that I'd better tell the truth or else. In the end I cracked."

"You confessed everything?"

Alexa nodded. "Dad was so angry. He swore I wasn't fit to keep horses and threatened to sell Dolly and her foal to the first people who came along. I begged him not to. But he stormed off again. Five minutes later I heard him on the phone to Jo Weston, saying he knew where Comanche was and that he was driving over to Hartfell to pick her up. That's the last I saw of him."

My Magical Pony

"So what did you do then?" Krista wanted to know. "Don't tell me – you rang Lee on his mobile and told him what had happened!"

"Yes. I said Dad was on the rampage. Then it was Lee's turn to panic. Dad doesn't like Lee, and this latest thing has made it much, much worse."

"So what did Lee do after that phone call?" Over the dull churn of the cement mixer, Krista picked up the sound of another car engine roaring up the lane.

"I guess he took Comanche and ran," Alexa groaned. "And this is Dad and Jo arriving now, and I don't know what on earth I'm going to tell them!"

Chapter Eleven

"Krista, come with me," Shining Star said quietly as Alexa hid her face in her trembling hands.

The car was coming closer. It turned on to the rough track.

Quickly Krista climbed on to his back. "Where are we going?" she asked.

"We're following these tracks through the heather," he answered, showing her a hoof print in the soft earth. "We will find Comanche."

So they left Alexa to face her angry father and trod along the ridge of the high hill

towards a large outcrop of black rocks. It wasn't long before they reached it.

"Listen," Star told her. "Do you hear anything?"

Krista strained to pick out any sound. There was the dry rustle of heather in the wind, and behind them the sound of car doors slamming then of voices being raised. She was about to shake her head when suddenly she heard a shuffling noise coming from behind the nearest rock. "Who's there?" she called quietly.

There was another movement of feet then a low whicker.

"Comanche!" Krista cried. She slid from Shining Star's back and ran behind the

boulder. She saw a dark-haired man scrambling away over the rocks, but she hardly noticed him, because here at last, standing steadfast and unafraid, was Comanche!

Krista didn't say a word as she flung both arms around the piebald pony's neck.

My Magical Pony

She hugged him and laid her face against his neck. He lowered his head and let out a long sigh.

Then Shining Star approached. "How quickly a sore heart is healed by an embrace," he said gently.

Krista looked up through happy tears. "Thank you so much, Star!"

Comanche was safe. He was sturdy as ever and the cut across his nose was starting to heal. He nudged Krista and stamped his feet. *What took you so long?* he seemed to say.

"And now shall we help Alexa and Lee?" the magical pony asked, gazing down the hill towards the ruined barn.

Krista frowned and hesitated.

"Even though they did wrong, they took good care of your friend here," Star reminded her.

Seeming to agree, Comanche gave Krista a nudge down the hill.

"OK," Krista agreed with a smile. "But how?"

As Comanche, Shining Star and Krista made their way down from the ridge, Star explained the problem. "Clive Barnes is an angry man. We must make his anger melt away and remind him that Alexa has a good heart."

"Easier said than done," Krista muttered, hearing voices yelling full blast.

"You've done some stupid things in your life, but this has to be the craziest yet!" Clive shouted.

My Magical Pony

Alexa had her hands to her ears. Jo Weston was standing between them, trying in vain to calm them down.

"That's it!" Clive decided. "I wash my hands of you, Alexa. And I'm telling you here and now that I'm not paying for the upkeep of your precious horses for one more day!"

"Dad, please!"

"Mr Barnes, calm down," Jo said, her eyes lighting up with relief when she caught sight of Krista walking down the hill with Comanche on one side and a grey moorland pony on the other. "Thank heavens!" she cried.

No – thank Shining Star! Krista thought. She beamed as Jo rushed up to Comanche and

gave him his second huge hug of the day.

Just then, Lee Harrison appeared from round the back of the barn. He ran towards Alexa's father and lunged at him. "Lay off her!" he shouted. "Can't you see what you're doing to her?"

Clenching his fists, Clive Barnes turned to face him. His face was red with fury. "Stay out of this, you layabout! This is between Alexa and me!"

"There's going to be a fight!" Krista gasped. As the situation slipped out of control, she turned to Shining Star for help. "Can you stop them?"

Star thought for a while. "All people are hasty and may be roused to anger," he replied

at last. "It is harder and it takes longer to make them look at the causes of their anger, so they may learn to forgive."

Krista nodded. "So how do we get the message through to Mr Barnes?"

"Watch," Shining Star replied calmly. "Let us see if I can bring out the best in the people here, for it lies deep within every living soul."

The magical pony arched his neck, spread his broad wings then stepped between the two men. Only Krista saw the cloud of silver mist which he breathed over the two angry men. Tiny, glittering drops of moisture surrounded them and for a moment hid them from view.

138

Red Skies

My Magical Pony

Alexa and Jo blinked. When they opened their eyes, it was as if a magician had waved his wand.

"Lee, I know your heart's in the right place," Clive Barnes began quietly. He'd lowered his fists and was looking shamefaced. "You may be a bit of a hothead, but then again I'm not exactly the easiest of blokes to get on with."

Alexa's eyes widened. She looked from her dad to Lee and back again.

"Yeah well, maybe I should've thought it through and tried to get Alexa to make things up with you," Lee muttered.

Clive stretched out his right hand. "Shake?"

Red Skies

With a nod, Lee ended the men's quarrel.

Then Clive Barnes turned to his daughter. The effects of Shining Star's glittering mist were not over yet. "I'm sorry, Alexa. I've not been myself lately – stress, problems with money and so on. But it was unfair of me to take it out on you."

Alexa put her hands to her mouth and shook her head in disbelief. "So you didn't mean what you said about Dolly and the foal?"

"Forget I ever said it," her father muttered.

"Well!" Jo whispered, holding Comanche's lead rope with one hand and scratching her head with the other. "Krista, am I hearing things, or did Clive, Lee and Alex just avoid one massive fight?"

My Magical Pony

Krista grinned. She stood with one arm around Star's neck. "You're not hearing things. They definitely stopped being angry and started making up."

"Amazing!" Jo murmured.

"And this means it is time for me to go," Shining Star told Krista.

So she walked with him up the hill, leaving Jo to make arrangements to take Comanche home.

"Don't be long, Krista!" Jo called after her. "It's nearly time for you to go to school!"

"Oh yes, school!" Krista sighed as she and Star reached the ridge. She looked back at Clive Barnes, deep in conversation with Alexa and Lee, and at brave Comanche

Red Skies

standing alongside his happy owner.

"And so goodbye," Shining Star said.

There were a dozen questions Krista wanted to ask before he flew away, but she only had time for one. "How did you do that?" she demanded. She watched him spread his beautiful wings and raise his head

to look up into the pale blue sky.

"Do what?" he asked, though he knew full well what she meant.

"How did you stop the fight? How did you take away the anger?"

He gazed fondly at her and beat his wings gently. "By magic," he replied, rising from the ground and giving her one last look.

"Sometimes, Krista, it is the only way!"